Stage Frightened

YEARLING BOOKS are designed especially to entertain and enlighten young people. Patricia Reilly Giff, consultant to this series, received her bachelor's degree from Marymount College and a master's degree in history from St. John's University. She holds a Professional Diploma in Reading and a Doctorate of Humane Letters from Hofstra University. She was a teacher and reading consultant for many years, and is the author of numerous books for young readers.

Stage Frightened

Judy Delton

Illustrated by Alan Tiegreen

A YEARLING BOOK

Published by
Bantam Doubleday Dell Books for Young Readers
a division of
Bantam Doubleday Dell Publishing Group, Inc.
1540 Broadway
New York, New York 10036

ISBN: 0-440-41327-3

Printed in the United States of America

August 1997

10 9 8 7 6 5 4 3 2 1

CWO

For Courtney Haefner, and her friends
Jessica, Amanda, and Shannon

Contents

CHAPTER 1

Double Good News

"Mrs. Peters," shouted Rachel Myers, "baby Nick is eating dirt!"

The Pee Wee Scouts were in their leader's backyard. It was a sunny day and all the Pee Wees except Roger White were playing croquet. Roger was digging up angleworms and putting them in Sonny Stone's Kool-Aid glass.

"Cut it out," shouted Sonny, chasing Roger with his croquet mallet.

"Nick is going to get tapeworm disease," said Mary Beth Kelly, who was

Molly Duff's best friend. "My mom says you get tapeworms from eating dirt. Or playing in a dirty sandbox."

"Then if Sonny drinks his Kool-Aid, he'll get it too," said Molly. "Angleworms live in dirt."

Mrs. Peters ran over to Nick and brushed him off. She wiped the dirt off his face with a Handi Wipe. Then she set him in his stroller, where he couldn't reach dirt.

Mrs. Stone, who was assistant troop leader, shook her finger at Roger and dumped out the glass with the worms.

Mrs. Peters clapped her hands. "It's time for our snack now," she said. "And then I have big news. News all of you will like!"

The Pee Wees hurried to pull up the cro-quet wickets and gather the mallets and balls. They liked snack time. And they liked good news.

"I hope this really is good news," said Tracy Barnes. "Sometimes Mrs. Peters thinks stuff is good news, but it's boring."

Tracy was right, thought Molly. Mrs. Peters often didn't know what was good news and what was bad news. Like the time she told them about earning a badge for writing to pen pals. Even though it had turned out all right, writing was too much like school to be fun.

"That library badge was a downer," said Tim Noon.

"It was not," said Kevin Moe, who liked to read. "Besides, you learned to read better when Molly helped you with words you didn't know."

"If it's a badge, I hope it's one where we go on a trip," said Patty Baker. She had a twin brother named Kenny.

4

"That last badge was fun!" said Jody George, remembering the trip to Center City, to the museum. Jody was Molly's favorite Pee Wee. He was smart and friendly, and he used a wheelchair.

In Center City the Pee Wees had played detective and identified the wrong man in their hotel as a criminal. It was embarrassing, but the train ride and hotel were lots of fun.

"Let's have our snack on the back deck today," said Mrs. Peters.

The Pee Wees sat at the picnic table. Mrs. Stone came out of the kitchen with glasses of cold milk and a big plate of cupcakes. Roger grabbed the biggest one and stuffed it into his mouth in two bites.

Ashley rolled her eyes. "He's disgusting," she said. "People in California have better manners than people in Minnesota." Ashley was Kenny and Patty's cousin from California. She was a tempo-rary Pee Wee Scout.

Molly felt cross with Ashley. Just be-cause Roger was rude didn't mean every-one in the state was. She was sure that people in California did rude things too. Her dad said they were fast drivers.

"Now for our good news," said Mrs. Peters, tying a bib around Nick's neck. "Actually it's double good news, and here is what it is."

CHAPTER 2

No-Talent Molly

"Is it a new badge?" asked Lisa Ronning. "Is that the good news?"

"It's part of it," said Mrs. Peters mysteriously.

The Pee Wees clapped and whistled and shouted. They all loved badges. They had lots of them. But they couldn't have too many, thought Molly. A badge was shiny and bright and colorful. It stood for something the Pee Wees had done together to have fun and help someone.

"Before I tell you what it is," said their

leader, "I have to tell you the other part of the news. I think you all heard about the new amusement park that just opened outside of town. It's called Minnesota Magic."

The Pee Wees cheered again. Mr. Duff had told Molly it was one of the biggest parks in the state. There were lots and lots of rides.

Rachel was waving her hand impatiently.

"Mrs. Peters! Mrs. Peters! I was there already. I went with my aunt."

Mary Beth groaned. "It figures," she said. "She goes to everything before anyone else."

"Well I thought it would be a nice trip for Troop Twenty-three," continued Mrs. Peters. "We could go and come back in one day, and ride on the rides, and have our lunch, and take in all the sights. They

say the roller coaster is as high as the sky.''

The Pee Wees really cheered now.

''It can't *really* be that high,'' said Kevin. ''They just say that to get people to ride on it.''

''It's high,'' said Rachel. ''My aunt said it was too high for us to go on. We went on the Ferris wheel instead.''

''It might not touch the sky,'' said Mrs. Peters, ''but it is high, and it is fun. The park is just right for a day's outing. There is only one problem—it costs money. Since we just got back from a trip to Center City, we have no money left to use. So I thought we could earn money to go to Minnesota Magic. And while we're earning money, we can be earning our new badge at the same time!''

This time the Pee Wees didn't cheer.

They waited to see if there was a catch. The park sounded fine, but what did their leader have in mind to earn money? And how could they earn money and a badge at the same time?

"We aren't selling doughnuts again, are we?" asked Tracy. "The powdered sugar makes me sneeze." Tracy had allergies.

"Is it a rummage sale?" asked Tim. "My mom says she has no more old stuff to donate."

"It's not rummage or doughnuts," said Mrs. Peters. "It's a talent show! I thought each Pee Wee could use his or her own talent to entertain others. We'd have a show and charge admission. We could all get a badge for doing what we do best, and the money from the audience will pay for the trip to the amusement park."

Molly felt her arms get covered with

goose bumps. She hated the word *talent*. Every time it came up it reminded her that she *had* no talent.

Rachel waved her hand and shouted, "Mrs. Peters, I have a problem."

Can it be that Rachel has no talent either? thought Molly.

"My problem is that I have so many talents I don't know which one to use," Rachel said.

The Pee Wees groaned.

"I could tap dance or do ballet, or I could sing or play the piano or the violin—how can I make up my mind which?"

Rachel looks more upset than she would if she had *no* talent, thought Molly.

"Big deal," muttered Tracy. "That doesn't sound like a problem to me."

"I'll leave that up to you," their leader said to Rachel. "I think there is plenty of talent in this group for each of you to entertain us for ten minutes. And there will be a wonderful reward at the end! A badge *and* a trip to the amusement park!"

Mrs. Peters held up a big calendar and circled one of the days in red.

"A Sunday would be a good day for the show," she said. "If we plan for the twenty-eighth of the month, it will give us plenty of time to choose what to do, and practice and perfect our acts. Then we'll put on the show at the elementary school."

All the Pee Wees began to talk at once.

"I'm glad I've been taking guitar lessons," said Jody. "I'm not very good, but I can play the same song I played in the recital."

"I've got a million talents," said Roger. "But my ventriloquist act will bring the house down. I don't even move my lips. It looks just like the dummy is talking."

"The dummy *is* talking," said Mary Beth to Molly. Roger heard her and threw a paper plate at her. Mary Beth ducked and it hit baby Nick, who began to cry. Mrs. Peters took Roger aside and spoke to him.

It seemed to Molly that everyone had a talent. Even Tim talked about showing everyone how to make tree ornaments out of old lightbulbs.

Molly didn't want everyone to know she had no talent. So after the meeting, she whispered it to Mrs. Peters.

"Don't worry, Molly," said their leader, "everyone has something they can do well. It can be any little thing. It doesn't have to be professional. You can just sing a little song or recite a poem."

But Molly couldn't carry a tune. Her

dad always teased her about singing off-key. It was one thing to sing off-key at a birthday party, but another thing to sing off-key on a big stage when people were actually paying money to hear her sing! No, singing was not a possibility.

And reciting a poem was for someone who had absolutely no real talent. Well, that's me, thought Molly, but I don't want to advertise it.

On the way home, everyone talked about their talents. Everyone except Molly.

"I'm going to do magic tricks," said Sonny. "I can pull a rabbit out of a hat and get out of handcuffs in five minutes. I can do some card tricks too."

"I'll believe it when I see it," said Lisa, rolling her eyes at Sonny. "Magic stuff takes years to learn."

"It didn't take *me* years," said Sonny.

Rat's knees, thought Molly, kicking a rock along the sidewalk. Even Sonny had a talent. Other people took lessons. Why didn't she? Her mother often suggested she learn to play the piano. And when the new ballet studio opened in town, her dad had said Molly would look fine in a tutu. Molly should have listened to them. Now she was left out again. Everyone had thought ahead to this day when talent would be called upon to earn a badge. Except Molly.

And now it was too late.

CHAPTER 3

Help Wanted

All week Molly looked for her talent. One by one, all the other Pee Wees decided what to do. Sonny practiced pulling scarves out of sleeves and tried to get a rabbit to come out of a hat.

Roger practiced talking without moving his lips.

Jody sat in his wheelchair and strummed his guitar whenever the Pee Wees got together.

Tim collected burned-out lightbulbs,

and Lisa had decided to do Japanese paper folding.

"My uncle lived in Japan," she said. "He showed me how."

Why didn't one of Molly's relatives live in Japan? Her relatives lived in Minnesota. Who could learn paper folding in Minnesota?

At the next Pee Wee meeting Mrs. Peters asked to hear the talent show plans. Everyone talked at once. Everyone except Molly.

"Kenny and Ashley and I are going to do a dance together," said Patty. "It's a sailor's hornpipe, and we even have costumes."

"I can't wait to see it!" said Mrs. Peters.

Molly was hoping Mary Beth would ask her to be in an act with her, since they were best friends. But Mary Beth didn't mention her plans, and Molly didn't want to ask.

Mrs. Peters had a pile of flyers to hand out. "Each of you take ten of these and pass them out to your relatives and friends," she said. "We want as many as possible to attend."

"My mom is going to put one up in her office," said Tracy.

"I think we should hang one in the drugstore and one in the bank," said Kevin, who had a businesslike mind.

"That's a good idea," said their leader.

Molly hoped no one she knew would see the flyer and come. They'd come to see her talent, and instead they'd see her do nothing. Zero. Zilch.

"I'm going to show everyone how to do different hairstyles," said Tracy. "My mom says I have a talent for working with hair."

Hair didn't sound like much of a talent to Molly, but it was surely better than *no* talent.

After the Pee Wees sang their song and said their pledge, Molly saw Roger walk up to Mrs. Peters's bulletin board and tack up a piece of paper. The writing was large. It said HELP WANTED. VENTRILOQUIST NEEDS A DUMMY. MUST SIT ON KNEE AND MOVE MOUTH. CALL ROGER WHITE.

Molly poked Mary Beth. "Look," she said. "Roger wants someone to be his dummy!"

"Who would do it?" said Mary Beth. "No one will answer *that* ad! But if they do, then they really *are* a dummy."

When Tracy saw Roger's note on the bulletin board, she scribbled something on a piece of paper and put it up beside his.

HELP WANTED, it said. HAIRSTYLIST NEEDS

SOMEONE'S HAIR TO FIX. CAN'T HAVE STAGE FRIGHT.
CALL TRACY BARNES.

When Roger read this, he got up and added something to his note. He added, DUMMY MUST NOT HAVE STAGE FRIGHT.

"I hate people fixing my hair," said Ashley. "Who would want those jobs? No one's going to apply."

Just then Sonny got up and ripped Roger's note down and said, "I'll take this job. How much does it pay?"

"It doesn't pay, dummy," said Roger. "You get to be onstage twice, that's your pay. Anyway, I have to interview all the guys that apply and then I decide."

"I wonder if I should take Tracy's job," said Mary Beth. "I like to get my hair fixed new ways."

Molly was thinking the same thing. It wouldn't be the same as a talent of her own. But it would be a way of being onstage. And maybe if she took both jobs, no one would notice that she had no talent!

"I'll take the job!" shouted Molly. "Both jobs!"

Everyone stared at Molly. This was the mark of a desperate Pee Wee! No one who could do anything on their own would do this. No one with an ounce of talent would sit on Roger's lap.

"You'll have to take a test," said Roger to Molly. "You and Sonny. To see who can move their mouth the best."

"I don't want a job that doesn't pay anything," said Sonny in disgust.

"I guess the job is yours," grumbled Roger to Molly. "I hope you can move your mouth fast and you aren't too heavy. I don't want my knee to get sore."

"You don't have to take a test for my job," said Tracy kindly. "I'll fix your hair in some great new way." Tracy looked at

Molly's hair. She frowned. "Your hair is kind of wiry, isn't it?" she said. "I may have to use some mousse on it. That's what my aunt does."

Molly wasn't sure she wanted mousse on her hair. And she knew she didn't want to sit on Roger's lap. What had she got herself into?

CHAPTER 4

Molly Finds a Talent (Too Late)

On the way home Mary Beth said, "I can't believe you're Roger's dummy!"

"I can't either," said Molly. "But I have no talent of my own!"

Mary Beth stared at her best friend. "You have lots of talent," she said.

"Name one thing," said Molly.

Mary Beth thought. "You make good lists," she said. "You're really good at planning things."

"Pooh," said Molly. "That's no talent. I can't stand on the stage and plan things."

"Well, it's writing talent," said Mary Beth. "You can make up rhymes and stories just like that!" Mary Beth snapped her fingers.

Mary Beth was right. Molly did like to write. Lists were only one of the things she wrote well.

"You could write a funny rhyme and read it," said Mary Beth.

"It's too late. I told Roger and Tracy I'd help them," said Molly. "I have to do it."

"Tell them you changed your mind," said Mary Beth.

But Molly always kept her word. Everyone said that about her. If she promised something, she did it. She did not back out. Rat's knees! Why had she been so quick to answer those ads?

27

When she got home, she told her parents the problem.

"You should keep your word," said her dad.

"Even though Roger usually doesn't keep his," her mother said, frowning.

"Why don't you write a funny poem anyway?" said her dad. "Then you get to be on the stage three times, you get a badge for your writing talent, *and* you get to go to Minnesota Magic. What could be more fun?"

When her dad put it that way, it made sense. Then why did Molly feel so worried? What could go wrong?

Before long, the talent show was only one day away. The flyers had paid off and ticket sales were brisk.

"We're almost sold out!" Mrs. Peters announced at the Pee Wee rehearsal.

Molly said she wouldn't sit on Roger's

knee for the rehearsal, just for the real thing.

"What if you're too heavy?" said Roger. "What if you break my knee?"

"Too bad," said Molly. She'd keep her word, but she wouldn't make it easy on Roger.

Rachel was dancing on tiptoe in her lavender tutu. Sonny was having trouble with a card trick. And Jody was trying a new song on his guitar that he had written himself. Jody has talent to spare, thought Molly. She wished she could borrow some of his.

Mary Beth had decided to dance the hornpipe with the Bakers, even if she wasn't part of their family.

"We really needed four," said Patty.

Rat's knees, why didn't they mention that *before* I signed up to be a dummy? thought Molly.

Molly had written four poems. She couldn't decide which one to use. One was about how much fun it was to be a Pee Wee Scout. Another was about earning badges. One was a nature poem, and one was about her dog, Skippy. Finally she decided on the Pee Wee Scout poem. She changed some words and then read it to her parents.

"I like it," said Mrs. Duff.

"That's my girl," said Mr. Duff. "The talented author and poet."

Molly giggled. Her dad would like anything she did. She hoped he would still be laughing after her three stage performances!

On the day of the show, it was cloudy. By the time Molly and her family left to go to the auditorium of the elementary school, it was pouring. Thunder boomed and lightning flashed. Molly wondered if it was a warning. An announcement of bad news. But what bad things could happen?

When they arrived, the auditorium was filled with ticket holders. It looked as if Mrs. Peters was right. There would be plenty of money to go to Minnesota Magic. Molly must have been mistaken about the storm warning.

Tracy came running up to Molly. "We go on first!" she said. "You have to get into this plastic smock, and I have to wet down your hair!"

Wet down her hair? Rat's knees! Molly didn't know she'd have to be onstage three times with dripping-wet hair!

While Tracy was spraying her hair with a laundry bottle, Roger ran up.

"We go on second," he said. "You're going to have to do a fast costume change offstage!" He held up a suit that looked as if it was for a clown. It had red suspenders, a bow tie with dots, and a hat with a small visor.

No way am I wearing that! thought Molly.

"Hey, you can't be my dummy with dripping-wet hair!" he shouted. "You're going to ruin my act!"

Molly had been right. The storm was a bad omen.

CHAPTER 5

Pee Wees Onstage

The lights on the stage were so bright that Molly could hardly see the audience. Mrs. Peters was announcing the acts, starting with Tracy's hair act. Molly was scared stiff. She had real stage fright.

The crowd applauded when Molly walked onstage, dripping water. She sat on a stool while Tracy combed through her wet hair.

"First," said Tracy to the audience, "I am going to show you a hairstyle called a fluff."

Tracy combed and brushed and brushed and combed. It felt to Molly as if she was combing her hair backward. She was! It took Tracy the hairdresser a long time to get the hairdo the way she wanted it. When the hair began to dry, Tracy took a can and sprayed some pink mousse onto her hand. It felt thick and gooey when she rubbed it on Molly's head.

Finally Mrs. Peters came out with a hair dryer. Tracy blew Molly's thick, gooey, pink hair dry. It felt to Molly as if her hair was standing up on end in chocolate syrup—but she had to be wrong. No hairdo stood straight up. And this was not *chocolate* mousse, after all!

By the time Tracy had finished drying the fluff, her time onstage was over. Mrs. Peters said she was sorry to say they had to move on to the next act, because Tracy's ten minutes was up.

The audience seemed to like Tracy's act. They were applauding loudly. Molly heard Roger whistling through his teeth.

"It's darling!" said Tracy to Molly. "You look so cute! You should wear this fluff all the time!"

When Molly got offstage, she saw herself in a mirror. Her hair was fluff, all right! It stood straight up in the air. Molly appeared to have three times as much hair as she really did have. It looked as if she was caught in a windstorm! When she tried to comb it down, it popped right back up.

"Hey," said Roger, "comb your hair. My hat won't fit on your head that way."

"I did comb it," said Molly, wanting to cry.

Roger was right. The hat didn't fit. It sat high on top of the fluff hairdo, not even

touching Molly's head! This whole thing was embarrassing.

But there was no time to think of her hair. Roger was rushing her into the dummy costume.

"Now, when I pretend to pull a string in the back of your neck, you move your mouth like you're talking," he said.

Mrs. Peters announced "our very own Pee Wee ventriloquist," and Roger pulled Molly onto the stage. He plopped her down on his knee. "Now don't move," he whispered loudly, and the audience laughed.

"You'll never guess what happened to me on the way to school," said Roger to Molly and to the audience.

"What?" asked Molly.

The whole roomful of people laughed and clapped.

"No, you aren't supposed to answer,

dummy!" said Roger. "You can't say 'what.' I answer without moving my lips! That's what ventriloquism is!"

This made the audience laugh even more loudly.

"It seems silly to me," said Molly. "I can talk better with my mouth open than you can with yours closed. Now what happened to you on the way to school?"

By now Molly could see her father bent over laughing, and his face was red.

Roger was red too. And he had forgotten his lines. He forgot the punch line of his own joke!

"Well?" said Molly. "We're waiting to hear what happened. Did you step on a crack and break your mother's back? Did you meet Little Jack Horner sitting in a corner? What happened?"

The more Molly talked, the more the audience laughed. And the more they

laughed, the more she talked! This was fun! It was fun being funny! And fun stealing the lines from Roger! And best of all, it made Molly almost forget that her hair was still standing straight up in the air.

"Next time, I'm saving my money and buying a real dummy!" said Roger. "One that isn't alive!"

Then Roger pushed Molly off his lap and got up and walked offstage. The audience seemed to think it was all part of the act and kept applauding.

"What a good show," shouted a man in the audience. Probably Roger's father, thought Molly.

"You two should win a prize for the funniest talent," said Mary Beth when Molly walked backstage. She stared at Molly's hair, but she didn't say anything.

People were telling Roger how good the act was too.

"They think he planned it," said Tracy.

"I have lots of talent," Roger was telling them.

"He has no talent," said Mary Beth in disgust. "If it wasn't for you, no one would have laughed."

The next act was Jody. He played and sang a song he wrote himself.

Then Tim showed how to make lightbulb ornaments.

Before Sonny could pull his rabbit out of the hat, it jumped out of a box and ran away. It ran off the stage and through the audience and out the door. Sonny ran after it. By the time he came back, Mrs. Peters had gone on to the next act, which was the hornpipe dancers.

"I think your poem is last," said Rachel to Molly. "Right after my ballet dance."

It meant Molly did not have much time. She took her comb and combed and combed. She wet her hair again and combed. But the fluff was there to stay. Instead of hearing my poem, the audience will be looking at my hair, thought Molly.

Lisa did her paper folding, and Rachel danced. Then Mrs. Peters said, "And now for the grand finale, we have Molly Duff, our own Pee Wee author, to read a poem she wrote."

There was nothing to do but go on.

CHAPTER 6

Encore! Encore!

The stage seemed very big to Molly. It's because I'm all alone this time, she thought. She had managed to get the dummy suit off and get back into her own clothes, but she could not get back into her own hair. The mousse had done its job. She was able to flatten down the top a little, but the rest was still sticking straight up. She would have to live with standing-straight-up hair forever, or have her head shaved.

" 'What Pee Wees Mean to Me,' " read

Molly. Her voice sounded loud and hollow, as if she were in a deep pit.

" 'Pee Wees are fun at Halloween. And at Christmas and days in between. Pee Wees are fun when we go on a trip. Or play tag or crack-the-whip.' "

"We don't play crack-the-whip," Molly heard Rachel whisper.

"She needed *whip* for the rhyme," said Kevin. "That's poetic license."

Good for Kevin, thought Molly. No one says a poem has to be *true.*

" 'We had fun at Camp Ghost-Away, and fishing with our dads in May.' "

"That was June," shouted Roger. "It was Father's Day."

Molly ignored Roger and went on. May, June, what was the difference? Molly wished Roger would try to write a poem. It wasn't easy.

" 'We skate and slide and swim and

rake, and when we're through we eat a cupcake. We help out others every day, and when we're through we get a badge.' "

The Pee Wees made faces. "That doesn't rhyme," shouted Sonny.

"No word rhymes with *badge*," Molly shouted back from the stage. *"It's not my fault."*

"*Madge* does," said Lisa. "I have an aunt named Madge. You could use her in your poem."

"But she isn't a Pee Wee, so how can she be in Molly's poem?" demanded Ashley.

Mrs. Peters clapped her hands, and Molly went on.

" 'The Pee Wees' days are very sunny, except sometimes with Roger and Sonny.' "

"Hey, we're in Molly's poem!" shouted Roger. "We're celebrities!"

" 'It's no fun when our meeting ends, but the best part of Pee Wees is doing stuff with friends.' The end."

Molly gave a little bow and walked off the stage. She had done it! It was over! It wasn't the greatest poem in the world, but she'd written it herself. And that took some talent.

Everyone clapped and whistled.

"That was great!" said Mary Beth when Molly came backstage. "My favorite line was the one about doing stuff with friends."

"Mine too," said Molly.

In the audience, people were shouting, "Encore! Encore!"

"That means they want more," said Jody.

"Who would like to do an encore?" asked Mrs. Peters with a worried look on her face. She's worried, thought Molly, that none of the Pee Wees has an encore.

"I can play another song," said Jody.

"Wonderful!" said their leader. And Jody took his guitar and wheeled himself back onto the stage while everyone clapped and clapped.

It turned out that most of the Pee Wees wanted to go back onstage!

"Rat's knees, I sure don't!" said Molly.

The Bakers and Mary Beth did their hornpipe all over again, and Rachel did another dance, a tap dance this time. Tim painted more ornaments, but Roger and Tracy did not volunteer, Molly noticed. Finally the encores were finished, and the Pee Wees all held hands and made a long line across the stage. They bowed several times.

Then, just before Mrs. Peters herded

them offstage, Molly's dad ran up to the stage with a flower for every Pee Wee.

"Just like in the real theater in New York," said Rachel, throwing kisses to the audience.

"Do we get our badges now?" Sonny asked Mrs. Peters.

"His magic show was kind of a flop," whispered Lisa to Molly. "I don't think he should get a badge!"

"Not tonight," said Mrs. Peters to Sonny. "I think we've all had enough excitement for one day. We need to get rested up for our big trip to Minnesota Magic. And I have to count our money to be sure we can afford it!"

The next day they found out that not only did they have plenty of money for the trip, but they also had money left over to put in the bank for future projects, like making baskets of food and gifts for the homeless or for children in the hospital at Christmas.

"I know one project I want to work on right away," said Molly to Mary Beth that afternoon.

"What?" asked her best friend. "Giving our talent show at the senior center?"

Molly shook her head. "That's not a bad idea," she said. "But mine is more important."

"Really?" said Mary Beth.

Molly nodded. "It's getting this darn mousse out of my hair!" she said. "I don't want to go to Minnesota Magic with my hair standing straight up!"

Mary Beth giggled. "I'll help," she said.

The girls got lots of shampoo—and they needed it. Molly leaned over the laundry tub in the basement, and after three shampoos, her hair finally agreed to lie down.

"Ahhhh," said Mr. Duff when they

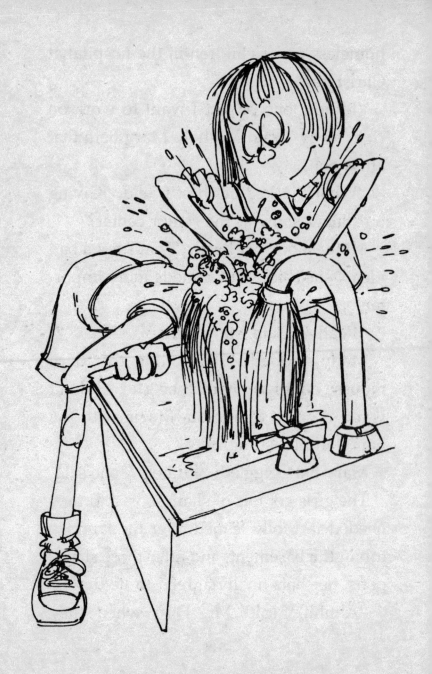

came upstairs. "I kind of miss the fluff. It gave you a windblown look."

The girls giggled. They knew he was kidding. No one, not even a person's own father, could like to look at someone with their hair standing straight up!

CHAPTER 7

All Aboard for Minnesota Magic!

The night before the big trip, it was hard for the Pee Wees to sleep. The thought of a roller coaster as high as the sky (even if it really wasn't) was scary. It gave Molly goose bumps, thinking about it!

In the morning the Pee Wees all met at Mrs. Peters's house. Mr. Peters and baby Nick were coming too. And some of the parents were coming to help out. It takes more than two adults to handle all of the

Pee Wees, thought Molly. On their last trip, Molly's parents had been helpers. She was glad they weren't coming along this time. Things just were not quite as much fun when your mom and dad were watching. Mary Beth's parents were coming, but she didn't seem to mind.

Mr. Peters checked to be sure they had first-aid equipment, emergency tools, and snacks for the drive. Then half the Pee Wees climbed into the Peterses' van, half into Mr. Kelly's station wagon, and they were on their way. They drove through their neighborhood, then across the Mississippi River, onto Highway 494, and out of town. Soon they got off the freeway and onto a country road. They went up one hill and down another and around two curves. Suddenly Jody shouted and pointed out the window.

"There it is, the Mile High roller coaster!"

Sure enough, Jody was right. Just looking at those tracks in the distance made Molly's stomach ache. It was definitely a mile high. It looked as if it touched the sky. Or at least a cloud.

And it was long. The cars on the track rose over the tops of the trees and then swooped down and disappeared behind buildings. Then the cars chugged up the track slowly and plunged down again.

"I'm not going on that thing," said Tracy. "I'm going on the bumper cars."

"Bumper cars are for babies," scoffed Sonny. "My little brother and sister go on them."

"You can go on bumper cars back home at our park," said Lisa to Tracy. "We have to try something daring and dangerous."

Molly felt the way Tracy did. She did

not want to go on the dangerous roller coaster.

"I read that it isn't really a mile high," said Jody to Molly as they got out of the van. "And it's not dangerous. If it were, they wouldn't let kids go on it."

Molly nodded, but she wasn't convinced. Even if it was perfectly safe, she didn't want to go near it. At the very least, it would make her stomach ache. At the worst, she would throw up. Or their car would get stuck a mile up in the air. Or she would fall out of the car as it was plunging downward around a curve. What if *all* those things happened?

"Let's sit together on the roller coaster," said Jody to Molly. "Okay?"

Just when Molly had made up her mind to avoid the roller coaster, Jody wanted her to sit with him! Now she was tempted to change her mind. How often did a boy you liked ask to sit with you on a scary ride?

Molly liked Jody. A lot. If Roger or Sonny had asked her, she'd have said no on the spot. But how could she say no to Jody? To ask someone to sit with you is a big deal. You don't ask someone you don't like to share one of those little seats.

Rat's knees! Why couldn't Jody have asked her to do something like share a seat on the Ferris wheel? Why did it have to be something so scary?

Molly heard herself say "Okay" to Jody.

"Good," he said.

Which meant that he was counting on her. If Molly changed her mind, he'd have to sit alone. Molly could not back out. She had said okay. Just like she had when she told Roger she'd be his dummy. She kept her word, even when she was scared stiff. Rat's knees. Why was she so dependable?

They pulled into the parking lot, which was already full of cars and buses. Mr. Peters pinned name tags on the Pee Wees, with the car license number and parking space number.

"In case anyone gets lost, just go to the grandstand," he said. He pointed to it. "We will find you there. But let's not have anyone wandering off today." He looked at Sonny and Roger. They pretended not to notice.

"First we'll take a boat ride around the park," said Mrs. Peters. "Then we'll go into the house of mirrors, and the haunted mansion, and then on the Ferris wheel."

"Is that the agenda, Mrs. Peters?" asked Kevin. Kevin liked to use big words.

"That's right, Kevin, that's the plan," laughed Mrs. Peters.

Mrs. Peters had not mentioned the Mile High roller coaster in her agenda. Maybe it was too high and too dangerous for children. Molly hoped that was the reason. Then she wouldn't have to go on it. But then she'd miss out sitting with Jody.

Jody was waving his hand. "Mrs. Peters," he said. "When are we going on the roller coaster?"

"Well, that ride is too scary for me," she said. "But for all the brave ones who like to be scared, I thought we'd do that this afternoon, after our lunch settles. I only hope we'll have some brave adults to go on it as helpers."

Molly wished Mrs. Peters had said "I think that ride is too scary for *any* of us to go on." Then she could tell Jody what bad luck it was. She could say, "Oh well, let's go on the Ferris wheel together instead."

But the roller coaster was on the agenda. And she couldn't tell Jody she was a big baby who had changed her mind. Besides, she wanted to sit with him in that little seat. It would be the bravest thing, the scariest thing, the hardest thing she ever did—and there wasn't even a badge for it! There should be a badge. A bravery badge.

The worst thing about it, outside of actually shooting down that great big high track, was thinking about it all day long. Molly would be unable to enjoy the haunted mansion or the house of mirrors or the Ferris wheel because she would be busy dreading the roller coaster.

Maybe she should come clean and tell Jody she was a chicken, or that heights made her dizzy, or that speed made her throw up. But then someone else would get to sit with him. Probably Rachel, who liked Jody too.

Rat's knees! It looked as if this would be a trip she'd never forget. For more than one reason.

CHAPTER 8

Scared Stiff

The Pee Wees broke up into two groups. Some went with Mr. and Mrs. Peters, and some went with the Kellys.

Molly and Mary Beth went with the Peterses. Mary Beth told Molly she didn't want to go with her own parents.

In the haunted mansion Sonny got so scared of a bodiless hand that Mr. Peters had to take him out.

"Well, it was a live hand without a body!" said Sonny. "Anybody would be scared stiff of that."

"No they wouldn't," said Mary Beth. "Only you."

Molly would have been having a very good time if it hadn't been for the roller coaster worry. That seemed to ruin the whole day. She finally told Mary Beth.

"I think you should tell Jody," said Mary Beth. "The truth is always best, my mom says."

But with Molly the truth was never that simple. Sometimes she didn't even know what *was* the truth and what wasn't. She looked at the other Pee Wees laughing and talking and having a good time. Why did she have to be so different? Why did she always worry about trouble? Didn't the others see problems all around them too?

On the Ferris wheel the seats were big enough for two. Molly and Mary Beth sat together. When they went over the top, Molly's stomach seemed to be left behind.

If the Ferris wheel was this bad, what would the roller coaster be like?

"I'm not going on that thing," she shouted to Mary Beth.

"Good," said Mary Beth. "I'd be scared stiff too. Come on the bumper cars with us instead."

Molly *was* scared stiff. But she wanted to sit with Jody. "I don't like bumper cars," she said.

"Well, you better make up your mind before Mr. Peters gets the tickets," said Mary Beth.

"I guess I'll do it," said Molly.

"Well, there's always the chance it will break down before it's your turn," said Mary Beth. "Maybe some little spring will pop out of something and you won't have to decide after all."

Mary Beth meant to make her feel better, Molly knew. But it only made her feel worse. Did roller coasters really have springs? How could a little spring keep a roller coaster from working?

And what if the spring didn't break *before* she and Jody got on, but *during*?

At lunchtime, after all the walking and exercise, the Pee Wees were starving.

All except Molly. Mr. Peters and Mr. Kelly went to a hotdog stand and brought back lots of good food to eat at a picnic table. The picnic table was on a grassy hill, with flowers all around and a good view of the roller coaster.

Whiz, grind, swooooosh! it went, as the Pee Wees munched their dogs.

Except Molly. Her dog and fries sat on her paper plate and got cold.

"Hey, can I have yours?" said Roger. His face was covered with mustard and ketchup.

Molly nodded, and Roger gobbled down a second lunch.

Molly sat on the grass and watched for a spring to pop off the roller coaster. She could picture it happening. And when it did, a voice would come over the loud-speaker saying, "We are sorry, but due to repairs, the roller coaster will be closed for the rest of the day. Money will be cheerfully refunded."

Molly was so lost in thought that she was sure it was real. She felt happy and relieved and didn't even hear Mary Beth talking to her.

"Hey, Mr. Peters is going to buy the tickets—you guys go on the roller coaster at one o'clock."

"It's closed," said Molly. "The roller coaster is closed for repairs."

But when she looked up, the roller

coaster was chugging up the track as it had done before. As she watched, it plunged down like lightning and everyone on it screamed!

"It isn't closed," said Mary Beth. "What's the matter with you?"

Mr. Peters asked how many wanted to ride, and when Molly saw Jody's hand go up in a flash, she forced hers up too.

Mr. Peters counted. "Six children and two adults, then," he said. He set off toward the ticket booth, and when he came back, he had the tickets. This was it. Molly was going to do the bravest thing of her life, and she wasn't even going to get a badge for it.

CHAPTER 9

A Surprise for Molly

After lunch Mrs. Peters led the Pee Wees to a big pavilion where there were deck chairs for people to sit in and watch the swimmers and boaters.

"We'll all have a little rest now," said their leader, "to let our lunch settle."

Molly's lunch didn't need to settle. Or at any rate, it needed to settle in Roger's stomach, not hers. Mary Beth lay next to her, snoring away. Molly wished she could fall asleep that easily.

"Do you know what?" said Rachel, who was on the other side of Molly. "Mrs. Peters said our new badge is for our talent. But don't you think we should get a badge for coming to an amusement park? And for going on the scary rides? I mean, I think since it's a two-part project, we should get two badges."

Rachel may be right, thought Molly. It's unusual not to earn a badge for a Pee Wee trip. Even a one-day trip. But no one mentioned another badge.

"I guess a trip is just for fun," said Rachel. "And you don't get a badge just for having a good time, do you?"

Rachel might think this trip was a good time, but it didn't feel that way to Molly. It felt as if she deserved a badge for all this worry. The worry was a lot more work than going onstage three times.

After a while Molly dozed off and

dreamed that the Pee Wees could earn badges only if they went to the top of the roller coaster to get them! High in the sky, Mrs. Peters stood on a fluffy cloud, like the pictures of God in Molly's grandma's prayer book, and gave them badges for having fun. Just as Molly was telling their leader she didn't deserve a badge because she was definitely not having a good time, she felt someone shaking her.

"Hey," said Jody. "It's time to go on the Mile High roller coaster!"

Was Molly's dream coming true?

"Have fun," called Mary Beth, waving to Molly and Jody as they left.

Fun, fun, fun, is that all anyone around here talks about? thought Molly.

Molly tried to walk slowly to delay the ride, but Jody's wheelchair seemed to be racing along. "We want to get a good seat!" he said.

"The seats are all alike," muttered Molly. Jody didn't hear her. He was already at the entrance, watching the cars pull to a stop to let the riders off. Molly joined Jody and Mary Beth's dad and Roger behind the rope that separated the people getting off from the people waiting to get on. Mr. Kelly pointed to the safety signs posted nearby.

" 'Remain seated in the cars while they are in motion,' " he read. " 'Fasten the seat belt firmly.' "

"Big deal," said Roger. "Those rules are for babies."

Mr. Peters glared. He took Roger aside and spoke to him quietly.

Molly and Jody watched people get out of the cars and walk down the ramp. One woman said, "Boy, I'll never go on *that* thing again." She leaned against the ticket booth and looked as if she might faint.

Three children were clinging to their fathers and crying as they climbed out of the cars.

Roger ignored them. He was waiting to dash onto the car he'd share with Mr. Peters. He wanted to sit in the front seat!

"It looks higher from up close, doesn't it?" Jody asked Molly.

Molly looked up. Her head swam, the tracks went so high. She nodded.

Jody was watching the rest of the riders stagger out of the cars. Most of them did not look happy.

So far, no springs had popped and no voice had said the roller coaster was out of order. It looked to Molly as if she'd have to bite the bullet, as her grandma said. There was no last-minute angel who was going to swoop down and save her. Well, she'd have to be brave and make the best of it.

And then, at the very last minute, just when the attendant unlatched the rope and Roger dashed through, a most unexpected thing happened. It was even better than a spring springing. Molly heard Jody's voice say to her very clearly, "I don't think I want to go on this ride after all."

CHAPTER 10

Badges for All

Molly couldn't believe her ears!

"I'm sorry to change my mind and ruin your fun," he said. "But it looks scarier than I thought. I guess everyone else has a partner by now. Could you sit alone?"

"It's fine!" Molly almost shouted. She thought about adding, "I didn't want to go on it anyway!" But she didn't. There was no need to make that confession. Her life was saved without it.

Jody leaned back in his wheelchair and looked white.

Molly gave Mr. Kelly the tickets and explained what had happened.

"Jody just got scared at the last minute," she said.

"That can easily happen," said Mr. Kelly. "I'll give the two tickets to someone who can use them."

Mr. Kelly wasn't even surprised! Molly herself could have changed her mind at the last minute, and no one would have cared! They would have understood. Why hadn't she?

Molly knew why. She didn't want the others to think she was afraid. Her dad had always said not to worry about what people thought if you knew you were doing the right thing. But Molly *did* worry about it.

Jody hadn't worried. He'd felt afraid and he'd changed his mind. Molly decided she would have to remember that. It was okay to change your mind and take care of yourself.

Molly and Jody joined the others watching the cars climb to the sky. No one made fun of Jody, and no one even teased him for changing his mind.

"I'm sorry you missed out on the ride," Jody said to Molly.

"No problem," said Molly. "I'd rather watch."

Those three words were probably the truest Molly had ever spoken.

All of a sudden, Molly felt very, very hungry! She asked Mrs. Peters if she could have a hotdog.

"I'd like one too, please," said Jody.

As they munched their late lunches, they watched Roger and the rest of the riders go up and down and over and under and sideways.

When the roller coaster stopped and

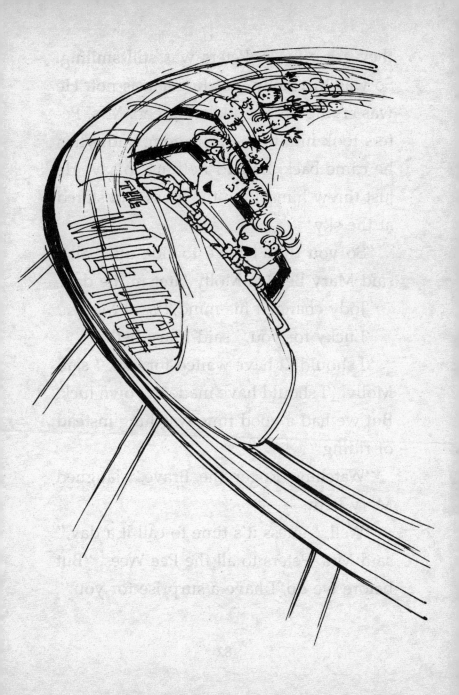

they got off, Mr. Peters was still smiling. So was Mr. Kelly. But Roger was not. He was crying and he looked green. Mrs. Peters took him to the rest room, and when he came back, he had nothing to say. He just threw himself on the grass and stared at the sky.

"So you didn't have to ride after all," said Mary Beth to Molly later in the day.

"Jody changed his mind," said Molly.

"Lucky for you," said Mary Beth.

"I shouldn't have waited for luck," said Molly. "I should have made my own luck. But we had a good time watching instead of riding."

"Watching Roger the Brave," laughed Mary Beth.

"Well, I guess it's time to call it a day," said Mrs. Peters to all the Pee Wees. "But before we do, I have a surprise for you."

"Another ride?" asked Tracy. Roger moaned.

"An ice cream cone?" asked Lisa.

"Neither of the above," said their leader, reaching into the bag of Pee Wee supplies. She took out a pile of little round shiny things.

"Badges?" said Rachel. "Are we getting our badges here at the park?"

"I thought it would be a good way to end our trip, and end our day," said Mrs. Peters. "A new badge is fun to get."

"More fun than being onstage, or even going on a roller coaster," whispered Molly to Mary Beth.

Mrs. Peters called names and gave each Pee Wee the talent badge he or she had earned.

"I think you all learned a lot by putting on a talent show," said Mrs. Peters. "You practiced your talents and then you were brave enough to go on a big stage and perform them in front of lots of people. You were afraid, but you did it anyway."

"I learned that it's okay to be scared," said Molly. She was thinking of the talent show *and* the roller coaster.

"Good for you, Molly," said Mrs. Peters. "And let's not forget there are times when it's okay to be afraid and *not* do something."

"I learned the roller coaster can make you sick," shouted Roger.

"And that was a good lesson even though it has nothing to do with the talent show," said their leader.

Mrs. Peters must have noticed that Jody was scared of the roller coaster and that he had stood up for himself and changed his mind, Molly thought.

"Mrs. Peters knows a lot," said Molly to Mary Beth.

The Pee Wees examined their new badges. They said the Pee Wee pledge. Then they sang the Pee Wee song.

And then, as the sun went down in the west, all the tired Pee Wees said goodbye to Minnesota Magic and climbed into the van for the trip home.

Molly curled up on the seat and thought about the day. "Rat's knees," she said to herself. Being a Pee Wee was sometimes not an easy thing to do. But it was still the best thing in town!

Pee Wee Scout Song

(to the tune of
"Old MacDonald Had a Farm")

Scouts are helpers, Scouts have fun,
Pee Wee, Pee Wee Scouts!
We sing and play when work is done,
Pee Wee, Pee Wee Scouts!

With a good deed here,
And an errand there,
Here a hand, there a hand,
Everywhere a good hand.

Scouts are helpers, Scouts have fun,
Pee Wee, Pee Wee Scouts!

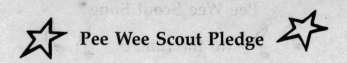

Pee Wee Scout Pledge

We love our country
And our home,
Our school and neighbors too.

As Pee Wee Scouts
We pledge our best
In everything we do.